WILLIAM
BOYD

KILLING LIZARDS
AND OTHER STORIES

PENGUIN BOOKS

PENGUIN BOOKS

Published by the Penguin Group. Penguin Books Ltd, 27 Wrights Lane,
London w8 5TZ, England. Penguin Books USA Inc., 375 Hudson Street,
New York, New York 10014, USA. Penguin Books Australia Ltd, Ringwood,
Victoria, Australia. Penguin Books Canada Ltd, 10 Alcorn Avenue, Toronto,
Ontario, Canada M4V 3B2. Penguin Books (NZ) Ltd, 182–190 Wairau Road,
Auckland 10, New Zealand · Penguin Books Ltd, Registered Offices: Har-
mondsworth, Middlesex, England · **These stories have been taken from *On the
Yankee Station* by William Boyd, first published by Hamish Hamilton in
1981 and published by Penguin Books in 1982.** This edition published 1995
Copyright © William Boyd, 1981. All rights reserved · Typeset by Datix International Limited, Bungay, Suffolk. Printed in England by Clays Ltd, St Ives plc ·
Except in the United States of America, this book is sold subject to the condition
that it shall not, by way of trade or otherwise, be lent, re-sold, hired out, or
otherwise circulated without the publisher's prior consent in any form of binding
or cover other than that in which it is published and without a similar condition
including this condition being imposed on the subsequent purchaser ·
10 9 8 7 6 5 4 3 2 1

CONTENTS

Killing Lizards

Gavin squatted beside Israel, the cook's teenage son, on the narrow verandah of the servants' quarters. Israel was making Gavin a new catapult. He bound the thick, rubber thongs to the wooden Y with string, tying the final knot tight and nipping off the loose ends with his teeth. Gavin took the proffered catapult and tried a practice shot. He fired at a small grove of banana trees by the kitchen garden. The pebble thunked into a fibrous bole with reassuring force.

'Great!' Gavin said admiringly, then 'hey!' as Israel snatched the catapult back. He dangled the weapon alluringly out of Gavin's reach and grinned as the small twelve-year-old boy leapt angrily for it.

'Cig'rette. Give me cig'rette,' Israel demanded, laughing in his high wheezy way.

'Oh, all right,' Gavin grudgingly replied, handing over the packet he had stolen from his mother's handbag the day before. Israel promptly lit one up and confidently puffed smoke up into the washed-out blue of the African sky.

Gavin walked back up the garden to the house. He was

a thin dark boy with a slightly pinched face and unusually thick eyebrows that made his face seem older than it was. He went through the kitchen and into the cool spacious living room with its rugs and tiled floor, where two roof fans energetically beat the hot afternoon air into motion.

The room was empty and Gavin walked along the verandah past his bedroom and that of his older sister. His sister, Amanda, was at boarding school in England; Gavin was going to join her there next year. He used to like his sister but since her fifteenth birthday she had changed. When she had come out on holiday last Christmas she had hardly played with him at all. She was bored with him; she preferred going shopping with her mother. A conspiracy of sorts seemed to have sprung up between the women of the family from which Gavin and his father were excluded.

When he thought of his sister now, he felt that he hated her. Sometimes he wished the plane that was bringing her out to Africa would crash and she would be killed. Then there would only be Gavin, he would be the only child. As he passed her bedroom he was reminded of his fantasy and despite himself he paused, thinking about it again, trying to imagine what life would be like – how it would be different. As he did so the other dream began to edge itself into his mind, like an insistent hand signalling at the back of a classroom drawing attention to itself. He had this dream quite a lot these days and it made him feel peculiar: he knew it was bad, a wrong thing to do, and sometimes he forced himself not to think about it. But it never worked, for it always came faltering back with its strange imaginative allure, and he would find himself lost in it, savouring its pleasures, indulging in its sweet illicit sensations.

It was a variation on the theme of his sister's death, but this time it also included his father. His father and sister had died in a car crash and Gavin had to break the news to his mother. As she sobbed with grief she clung to him for support. Gavin would soothe her, stroking her hair as he'd seen done on TV in England, whispering words of comfort.

In the dream Gavin's mother never remarried, and she and Gavin returned to England to live. People would look at them in the street, the tall elegant widow in black and her son, growing tall and more mature himself, being brave and good by her side. People around them seemed to whisper, 'I don't know what she would have done without him' and 'Yes, he's been a marvel' and 'They're so close now'.

Gavin shook his head, blushing guiltily. He didn't hate his father – he just got angry with him sometimes – and it made him feel bad and upset that he kept on imagining him dead. But the dream insistently repeated itself, and it continued to expand; the narrative furnished itself with more and more precise details; the funeral scene was added, the cottage Gavin and his mother took near Canterbury, the plans they made for the school holidays. It grew steadily more real and credible – it was like discovering a new world – but as it did, so Gavin found himself more and more frustrated and oppressed by the truth, more dissatisfied with the way things were.

Gavin slowly pushed open the door of his parents' bedroom. Sometimes he knocked, but his mother had laughed and told him not to be silly. Still, he was cautious as he had once been horribly embarrassed to find them both asleep, naked and sprawled on the rumpled double bed. But today he knew his father was at work in his chemistry lab. Only his mother would be having a siesta.

But Gavin's mother was sitting in front of her dressing table brushing her short but thick reddish auburn hair. She was wearing only a black bra and pants that contrasted strongly with the pale freckly tan of her firm body. A cigarette burned in an ashtray. She brushed methodically and absentmindedly, her shining hair crackling under the brush. She seemed quite unaware of Gavin standing behind her, looking on. Then he coughed.

'Yes, darling, what is it?' she said without looking round.

Gavin sensed rather than appreciated that his mother was a beautiful woman. He did not realize that she was prevented from achieving it fully by a sulky turn to her lips and a hardness in her pale eyes. She stood up and stretched languidly, walking bare-footed over to the wardrobe where she selected a cotton dress.

'Where are you going?' Gavin asked without thinking.

'Rehearsal, dear. For the play,' his mother replied.

'Oh. Well, I'm going out too.' He left it at that. Just to see if she'd say anything this time, but she seemed not to have heard. So he added, 'I'm going with Laurence and David. To kill lizards.'

'Yes, darling,' his mother said, intently examining the dress she had chosen. 'Do try not to touch the lizards, they're nasty things, there's a good boy.' She held the dress up in front of her and looked at her reflection critically in the mirror. She laid the dress on the bed, sat down again and began to apply some lipstick. Gavin looked at her rich red hair and the curve of her spine in her creamy back, broken by the dark strap of her bra, and the three moles on the curve of her haunch where it was tautened by the elastic of her pants. Gavin swallowed. His mother's presence in his life loomed like a huge wall at whose foot his needs cowered like beggars at a city gate. He wished she bothered about him more, did things with him as she did with Amanda. He felt strange and uneasy about her, proud and uncomfortable. He had been pleased last Saturday when she took him to the pool in town, but then she had worn a small bikini and the Syrian men round the bar had stared at her. David's mother always wore a swimsuit of a prickly material with stiff bones in it. When he went out of the room she was brushing her hair again and he didn't bother to say good-bye.

Gavin walked down the road. He was wearing a striped T-shirt, white shorts and Clarks sandals without socks. The early afternoon sun beat down on his head and the heat vibrated up from the tarmac. On either side of him were the low senior-staff bungalows, shadowy beneath their wide eaves, and which seemed to be pressed down into the earth as if the blazing sun bore down with intolerable weight. The coruscating scarlet dazzle of flamboyant trees that lined the road danced spottily in his eyes.

The university campus was a large one but Gavin had come to know it intimately in the two years since his parents had moved to Africa. In Canterbury his father had only been a lecturer but here he was a professor in the Chemistry Department. Gavin loved to go down to the labs with their curious ammoniacal smells, brilliant fluids and mad-scientist constructions of phials, test-tubes and rubber pipes. He thought he might pay his father a surprise visit that afternoon as their lizard hunt should take them in that direction.

Gavin and his two friends had been shooting lizards with their catapults for the three weeks of the Easter holidays and had so far accounted for one hundred and forty-three. They killed mainly the male and female of one species that seemed to populate every group of boulders or area of concrete in the country. The lizards were large, sometimes growing to eighteen inches in length. The females were slightly smaller than the males and were a dirty speckled khaki colour. The males were more resplendent, with brilliant orange-red heads, pale grey bodies and black-barred feet and tails. They did no one any harm; just basked in the sun doing a curious bobbing press-up motion. At first they were ludicrously easy to kill. The boys could creep up to within three or four feet and with one well-placed stone reduce the basking complacent lizard to a writhing knot, its feet clawing at a buckled spine or shattered head. A slight guilt had soon grown up among the boys and they accordingly convinced themselves that the lizards were pests and that, rather like rats, they spread diseases.

But the lizards, like any threatened species, grew wise to the hunters and now scurried off at the merest hint of 7 approach, and the boys had to range wider and wider through the campus to find zones where the word had not spread and where the lizards still clung unconcernedly to walls, like dozing sunbathers unaware of the looming thunderclouds.

Gavin met his friends at the pre-arranged corner. Today they were heading for the university staff's preparatory school at a far edge of the campus. There was an expansive outcrop of boulders there with a sizeable lizard community that they had been evaluating for some time, and this afternoon they planned a blitz.

They walked down the road firing stones at trees and clumps of bushes. Gavin teased Laurence about his bandy legs and then joined forces with him to mock David about his spots and his hugely fat sister until he threatened to go home. Gavin felt tense and malicious, and lied easily to them about how he had fashioned his own catapult, which was far superior to their clumsier home-made efforts. He was glad when they rounded a corner and came in sight of the long simple buildings of the chemistry labs.

'Let's go and see my Dad,' he suggested.

Gavin's father was marking exam papers in an empty lab when the three boys arrived. He was tall and thin with sparse black hair brushed across his balding head. Gavin possessed his similar tentative smile. They chatted for a while, then Gavin's father showed them some frozen nitrogen. He picked a red hibiscus bloom off a hedge outside and dipped it in the container of fuming liquid. Then he dropped the flower on the floor and it shattered to pieces like fine china.

'Where are you off to?' he asked as the boys made ready to leave.

'Down to the school to get lizards,' Gavin replied.

'There's a monster one down there,' said David. 'I've seen it.'

'I hope you don't leave them lying around,' Gavin's father said. 'Things rot in this sun very quickly.'

'It's okay,' Gavin affirmed brightly. 'The hawks soon get them.'

Gavin's father looked thoughtful. 'What's your mother doing?' he asked his son. 'Left her on her own, have you?'

'Israel's there,' Gavin replied sullenly. 'But anyway she's going to her play rehearsal or something. Drama, drama, you know.'

'Today? Are you sure?' his father asked, seemingly surprised.

'That's what she said. Bye, Dad, see you tonight.'

The school lay on a small plateau overlooking a teak forest

and the jungle that stretched away beyond it. The outcrop of rocks was poised on the edge of the plateau and it ran down in pale pinkish slabs to the beginning of the teak trees.

The boys killed four female lizards almost at once but the others had rushed into crevices and stayed there. Gavin caught a glimpse of a large red-head as it scuttled off and the three of them pelted the deep niche it hid in and prodded at it with sticks, but it was just not coming out.

Then Gavin and Laurence thought they saw a fruit bat in a palm tree, but David couldn't see it and soon lost interest. They patrolled the deserted school buildings for a while and then hung, bat-like themselves, on the Jungle-Jim in the playground. David, who had perched on the top, heard the sound of a car as it negotiated a bumpy rutted track that led into the jungle and which ran for a while along the base of the plateau. He soon saw a Volkswagen van lurching along. A man was driving and a woman sat beside him.

'Hey, Gavin,' David said without thinking. 'Isn't that your mother?'

Gavin climbed quickly up beside him and looked.

'No,' he said. 'Nope. Definitely.'

They resumed their play but the implication hung in the air like a threat, despite their suddenly earnest jocularity. In the unspoken way in which these things arrange themselves, David and Laurence soon announced that they had to go home. Gavin said that he would stay on a bit. He wanted to see if he could get that big lizard.

Laurence and David wandered off with many a backward shouted message about where they would meet tomorrow and what they would do. Then Gavin clambered about half-heartedly on the Jungle-Jim before he walked down the slope to the track which he followed into the teak forest. There was still heat in the afternoon sun and the trees and bushes looked tired from a day's exposure. The big soup-plate leaves of the teak trees hung limply in the damp dusty atmosphere.

Gavin heard his mother's laugh before he saw the van. He moved off the track and followed the curve of a bend until he saw the van through the leaves. It was pulled up on the other side of the mud road. The large sliding door was thrown back and Gavin could see that the bunk bed inside had been folded down. His mother was sitting on the edge of the bunk, laughing. A man without a shirt was struggling to zip up her dress. She laughed again, showing her teeth and throwing back her head, joyously shaking her thick red hair. Gavin knew the man: he was called Ian Swan and sometimes came to the house. He had a neat black beard and curling black hair all over his chest.

Gavin stood motionless behind the thick screen of leaves and watched his mother and the man. He knew at once what they had been doing. He watched them caper and kiss and laugh. Finally Gavin's mother tugged herself free and scrambled round the van and into the front seat. Gavin saw a pair of sunglasses drop from her open handbag. She didn't notice they had fallen. Swan put on his shirt and joined her in the front of the van.

As they backed and turned the van Gavin held his breath in an agony of tension in case they should run over the glasses. When they had gone he stood for a while before walking over and picking up the sunglasses. They were quite cheap; Gavin remembered she had bought them last leave in England. They were favourites. They had pale blue lenses and candy-pink frames. He held them carefully in the palm of his hand as if he were holding an injured bird.

MUMMY . . .

As he walked down the track to the school the numbness, the blank camera stare that had descended on him the moment he had heard his mother's high laugh, began to dissipate. A slow tingling charge of triumph and elation began to infuse his body.

12   OH, MUMMY, I THINK . . .

He looked again at the sunglasses in his palm. Things would change now. Nothing would be the same after this secret. It seemed to him now as if he were carrying a ticking bomb.

OH, MUMMY, I THINK I'VE FOUND YOUR SUNGLASSES.

The lowering sun was striking the flat rocks of the outcrop full on and Gavin could feel the heat through the soles of his sandals as he walked up the slope. Then, ahead, facing away from him, he saw the lizard. It was catching the last warmth of the day, red head methodically bobbing, sleek torso and long tail motionless. Carefully Gavin set down the glasses and took his catapult and a pebble from his pocket. Stupid lizard, he thought, sunbathing, head bobbing like that, you never know who's around. He drew a bead on it, cautiously easing the thick rubber back to full stretch until his rigid left arm began to quiver from the tension.

He imagined the stone breaking the lizard's back, a pink welling tear in the pale scaly skin. The curious slow-motion way the mortally wounded creatures keeled over, sometimes a single leg twitching crazily like a spinning rear wheel on an upended crashed car.

The lizard basked on, unaware.

Gavin eased off the tension. Holding his breath with the effort, heart thumping in his ears. He stood for a few seconds letting himself calm down. His mother would be home now, he should have enough time before his father returned. He picked up the sunglasses and backed softly away and around leaving the lizard undisturbed. Then, with his eyes alight and gleaming beneath his oddly heavy brows, he set off steadily for home.

Not Yet, Jayette

This happened to me in LA once. Honestly. I was standing at a hamburger kiosk on Echo Park eating a chilé-dog. This guy in a dark green Lincoln pulls up at the kerb in front of me and leans out of the window. 'Hey,' he asks me, 'do you know the way to San José?' Well, that threw me, I had to admit it. In fact I almost told him. Then I got wise. 'Don't tell me,' I says. 'Let me guess. You're going back to find some peace of mind.' I only tell you this to give you some idea of what the city is like. It's full of jokers. And that guy, even though I'd figured him, still bad-mouthed me before he drove away. That's the kind of place it is. I'm just telling you so's you know my day is for real.

Most mornings, early, I go down to the beach at Santa Monica to try and meet Christopher Isherwood. A guy I know told me he likes to walk his dog down there before the beach freaks and the surfers show up. I haven't seen him yet but I've grown to like my mornings on the beach. The sea has that oily sheen to it, like an empty swimming pool. The funny thing is, though, the Pacific Ocean nearly always looks cold. One morning someone was swinging on the bars, up and down, flinging himself about as if he was made of rubber. It was beautiful, and boy, was he built. It's wonderful to me what the human body can achieve if you treat it right. I like to keep in shape. I work out. So most days I hang around waiting to see if Christopher's going to show then I go jogging. I head south; down from the pier to Pacific Ocean Park. I've got to know some of the bums that live around the beach, the junkies and derelicts. 'Hi, Charlie,' they shout when they see me jogging by.

There's a café in Venice where I eat breakfast. A girl works there most mornings, thin, bottle-blonde, kind of tired-looking. I'm pretty sure she's on something heavy. So that doesn't make her anything special but she can't be more than eighteen. She knows my name, I don't know how, I never told her. Anyway each morning when she brings me my coffee and doughnut she says 'Hi, there, Charlie. Lucked-out yet?' I just smile and say 'Not yet, Jayette.' Jayette's the name she's got sewn across her left tit. I'm not sure I like the way she speaks to me – I don't exactly know what she's referring to. But seeing how she knows my name I think it must be my career she's talking about. Because I used to be a star, well, a TV star anyway. Between the ages of nine and eleven I earned twelve thousand dollars a week. Perhaps you remember the show, a TV soap opera called 'The Scrantons'. I was the little brother, Chuck. For two years I was a star. I got the whole treatment: my own trailer, chauffeured limousines, private tutors. Trouble was my puberty came too early. Suddenly I was like a teenage gatecrasher at a kids' party. My voice went, I got zits all over my chin, fluff on my lip. It spoilt everything. Within a month the scenario for my contractual death was drawn up. I think it was pneumonia, or maybe an accident with the thresher. I can't really remember, I don't like to look back on those final days.

Though I must confess it was fun meeting all the stars. The big ones: Jeanne Lamont, Eddy Cornelle, Mary and Marvin Keen – you remember them. One of the most bizarre features of my life since I left the studio is that nowadays I never see stars any more. Isn't that ridiculous? Someone like me who worked with them, who practically lives in Hollywood? Somehow I never get to see the stars any more. I just miss them. 'Oh, he left five minutes ago, bub,' or 'Oh, no, I think she's on location in Europe, she hasn't been here for weeks.' The same old story.

I think that's what Jayette's referring to when she asks if I've lucked-out. She knows I'm still hanging in there, waiting. I mean, I've kept on my agent. The way I see it is that once you've been in front of the cameras something's going to keep driving you on until you get back. I 17 know it'll happen to me again one day, I just have this feeling inside.

After breakfast I jog back up the beach to where I left the car. One morning I got to thinking about Jayette. What does she think when she sees me now and remembers me from the days of 'The Scrantons'? It seems to me that everybody in their life is at least two people. Once when you're a child and once when you're an adult. It's the saddest thing. I don't just mean that you see things differently when you're a child – that's something else again – what's sad is that you can't seem to keep the personality. I know I'm not the same person any more as young Chuck Scranton was, and I find that depressing. I could meet little Charlie on the beach today and say 'Look, there goes a sharp kid.' And never recognize him, if you see what I mean. It's a shame.

I don't like the jog back so much, as all the people are coming out. Lying around, surfing, cruising, scoring, shooting up, tricking. Hell, the things I've seen on that sand, I could tell you a few stories. Sometimes I like to go down to El Segundo or Redondo beach just to feel normal.

I usually park the car on Santa Monica Palisades. I tidy up, change into my clothes and shave. I have a small battery-powered electric razor that I use. Then I have a beer, wander around, buy a newspaper. Mostly I then drive north to Malibu. There's a place I know where you can get a fair view of a longish stretch of the beach. It's almost impossible to get down there in summer; they don't like strangers. So I pull off the highway and climb this small dune-hill. I have a pair of opera glasses of my aunt's that I use to see better – my eyesight's not too hot. I spotted Rod Steiger one day, and Jane Fonda I think but I can't be sure, the glasses tend to fuzz everything a bit over four hundred yards. Anyway I like the quiet on that dune, it's restful.

I have been down on to Malibu beach, but only in the winter season. The houses are all shut up but you can still get the feel of it. Some people were having a bar-b-q one day. It looked good. They had a fire going on a big porch that jutted out high over the sand. They waved and shouted when I went past.

Lunch is bad. The worst part of the day for me because I have to go home. I live with my aunt. I call her my aunt though I'm not related to her at all. She was my mother's companion – I believe that's the right word – until my mother stuffed her face with a gross of Seconal one afternoon in a motel at Corona del Mar. I was fifteen then and Vanessa – my 'aunt' – became some kind of legal guardian to me and had control of all the money I'd made from 'The Scrantons'. Well, she bought an apartment in Beverly Glen because she liked the address. Man, was she swallowed by the realtor. They build these tiny apartment blocks on cliff-faces up the asshole of the big-name canyons just so you can say you live off Mulholland Drive or in Bel Air. It's a load. I'd rather live in Watts or on Imperial highway. I practically have to rope-up and wear crampons to get to my front door. And it is mine. I paid for it.

Maybe that's why Vanessa never leaves her bed. It's just too much effort getting in and out of the house. She just stays in bed all day and eats, watches TV and feeds her two dogs. I only go in there for lunch; it's my only 'family' ritual. I take a glass of milk and a salad sandwich but she phones out for pizza and enchiladas and burgers – any kind of crap she can smear over her face and down her front. She's really grown fat in the ten years since my mother bombed out. But she still sits up in bed with those hairy yipping dogs under her armpits, and she's got her top and bottom false eyelashes, her hairpiece and purple lipstick on. I say nothing usually. For someone who never gets out she sure can talk a lot. She wears these tacky satin and lace peignoirs, shows half her chest. Her breasts look like a couple of Indian clubs rolling around under the shimmer. It's unfair I suppose, but when I drive back into the foothills I like to think I'm going to have a luncheon date with . . . with someone like Grace Kelly – as was – or maybe Alexis Smith. I don't know. I wouldn't mind a meal and a civilized conversation with some nice people like that. But lunch with Vanessa? Thanks for nothing, pal. God, you can keep it. She's a real klutz. I'm sure Grace and Alexis would never let themselves get that way – you know, like Vanessa's always dropping tacos down her cleavage or smearing mustard on her chins.

I always get depressed after lunch. It figures, I hear you say. I go to my room and sometimes I have a drink (I don't smoke, so dope's out). Other days I play my guitar or else work on my screenplay. It's called 'Walk. Don't Walk'. I get a lot of good ideas after lunch for some reason. That's when I got the idea for my screenplay. It just came to me. I remembered how I'd been stuck one day at the corner of Arteria boulevard and Normandie avenue. There was a pile of traffic and the pedestrian signs were going berserk. 'Walk' would come on so I'd start across. Two seconds later 'Don't Walk' so I go back. Then on comes 'Walk' again. This went on for ten minutes: 'Walk. Don't Walk. Walk. Don't Walk.' I was practically out of my box. But what really stunned me was the way I just stayed there and obeyed the goddam machine for so long – I never even thought about going it alone. Then one afternoon after lunch it came to me that it was a neat image for life; just the right kind of metaphor for the whole can of worms. The final scene of this movie is going to be a slow crane shot away from this malfunctioning traffic sign going 'Walk. Don't Walk.' Then the camera pulls further up and away in a helicopter and you see that in fact the whole city is fouled up because of this one sign flashing. They don't know what to do; the programming's gone wrong. It's a great final scene. Only problem is I'm having some difficulty writing my way towards it. Still, it'll come, I guess.

In the late afternoon I go to work. I work at the Beverly Hills Hotel. Vanessa's brother-in-law got me the job. I park cars. I keep hoping I'm going to park the car of someone really important. Frank – that's Vanessa's brother-in-law – will say to me 'Give this one a shine-up, Charlie, it belongs to so and so, he produced this film,' or 'That guy's the money behind X's new movie,' or 'Look out, he's Senior Vice-President of Something incorporated.' I say big deal. These guys hand me the keys – they all look like bank clerks. If that's the movies nowadays I'm not so sure I want back in.

Afternoons are quiet at the hotel so I catch up on my reading. I'm reading Camus at the moment but I think I've learnt all I can from him so I'm going on to Jung. I don't know too much about Jung but I'm told he was really into astrology which has always been a pet interest of mine. One thing I will say for quitting the movies when I did means that I didn't miss out on my education. I

hear that some of these stars today are really dumb; you

know, they've got their brains in their neck and points south.

After work I drive back down to the Santa Monica pier and think about what I'm going to do all night. The Santa Monica pier is a kind of special place for me: it's the last place I saw my wife and son. I got married at seventeen and was divorced by twenty-two, though we were apart for a couple of years before that. Her name was Harriet. It was okay for a while but I don't think she liked Vanessa. Anyway, get this. She left me for a guy who was the assistant manager in the credit collection department of a large mail order firm. I couldn't believe it when she told me. I said to her when she moved out that it had to be the world's most boring job and did she know what she was getting into? I mean, what sort of person do you have to be to take on that kind of work? The bad thing was she took my son Skiff with her. It's a dumb name I know, but at the time he was born all the kids were being called things like Sky and Saffron and Powie, and I was really sold on sailing. I hope he doesn't hold it against me.

The divorce was messy and she got custody, though I'll never understand why. She had left some clothes at the house and wanted them back so she suggested we meet at the end of the Santa Monica pier for some reason. I didn't mind, it was the impetuous side to her nature that first 23 attracted me. I handed the clothes over. She was a bit tense. Skiff was running about; he didn't seem to know who I was. She was smoking a lot; those long thin menthol cigarettes. I really didn't say anything much at all, asked her how she was, what school Skiff was going to. Then she just burst out 'Take a good look, Charlie, then don't come near us ever again!' Her exact words. Then they went away.

So I go down to the end of the pier most nights and look out at the ocean and count the planes going in to land at LA International and try to work things out. Just the other evening I wandered up the beach a way and this thin-faced man with short grey hair came up to me and said 'Jordan, is that you?' And when he saw he'd made a mistake he smiled a nice smile, apologized and walked off. It was only this morning that I thought it might have been Christopher Isherwood himself. The more I think about it the more convinced I become. What a perfect opportunity and I had to go and miss it. As I say: 'Walk. Don't Walk.' That's the bottom line.

I suppose I must have been preoccupied. The pier brings back all these memories like some private video-loop, and my head gets to feel like it's full of birds all flapping around trying to get out. And also things haven't been so good lately. On Friday Frank told me not to bother showing up at the hotel next week, I can't seem to make any headway with the screenplay and for the last three nights Vanessa's tried to climb into my bed.

Well, tonight I think I'll drive to this small bar I know on Sunset. Nothing too great, a little dark. They do a nice white wine with peach slices in it, and there's some topless, some go-go, and I hear tell that Bobby de Niro sometimes shows up for a drink.

'Think of it,' Holland said. 'The sex.'

'Sex.' Panton repeated. 'God . . . Sex.'

Niles shook his head. 'Are you sure?' he asked. 'I mean, can you guarantee it? The sex, that is. I don't want to waste time farting around singing.'

'Waste bloody time? Are you mad?' Holland said. 'It only happens every two years. You can't afford to miss the opportunity. Unless you're suffering from second thoughts.'

'What, *me*?' Niles tried to laugh. He looked at Holland's blue eyes. They always seemed to know. 'You must be bloody kidding, mate. Jesus, if you think . . . God!' he snorted.

'All right, all right,' Holland said. 'We agreed, remember? It's got to be all of us.'

Niles had never asked for this last fact to be explained. Why – if, as Holland attested – the sex was freely available, on a plate so to speak, why did they all have to participate at the feast? Holland made out it was part of his naturally generous personality. It was more fun if you all had a go.

26   'Let's get on with it,' Panton said.

They walked over to the noticeboard. Holland pushed some juniors out of the way. Prothero, the music master, had written on the top of a sheet of paper: GILBERT AND SULLIVAN OPERA – HMS PINAFORE – CHORUS: BASSES AND TENORS WANTED, SIGN BELOW. Half a dozen names had been scrawled down.

'Cretins,' Holland said. 'No competition.' He wrote his name down. Panton followed suit.

Niles took a biro from his blazer pocket. He paused.

'But how can you be so sure? That's what I want to know. How can you tell that the girls just won't be – well – music-lovers?'

'Because I know,' Holland said patiently. 'Every Gilbert and Sullivan it's the same. Borthwick told me. He was in the last one. He said the girls only come for one thing. I mean, it stands to reason. What sort of girl's going to want to be in some pissing bloody operetta? Ask yourself. Shitty orchestra, home-made costumes, people who can't sing to save their life. I tell you, Nilo, they're doing it for the same reason as us. They're fed up with the local yobs. They want a nice public school boy. Christ, you must have heard. It's a cert. Leave it to Pete.'

Niles screwed up his eyes. What the hell, he thought, it's time I tried. He signed his name. Q. Niles.

'Good old Quentin,' Panton roared. 'Wor! Think of it waiting.' He forced his features into a semblance of noble suffering, wrapped his arms around himself as if riven with acute internal pain and lurched drunkenly about, groaning in simulated ecstasy.

Holland grabbed Niles by the arm. 'The shafting, Nilo my man,' he said intensely. 'The royal bloody shafting we're going to do.'

Niles felt his chest expand with sudden exhilaration. Holland's fierce enthusiasm always affected him more than Panton's most baroque histrionics.

'Bloody right, Pete,' he said. 'Too bloody right. I'm getting desperate already.'

Niles sat in his small box-like study and stared out at the relentless rain falling on the gentle Scottish hills. From his study window he could see a corner of the dormitory wing of his own house, an expanse of gravel with the housemaster's car parked on it and fifty yards of the drive leading down to the main school house a mile or so away. On the desk in front of him lay a half-completed team list for the inter-house rugby leagues and an open notepad. On the notepad he had written: *The Rape of the Lock*, and below that '*The Rape of the Lock* is a mock heroic poem. What do you understand by this term? Illustrate with examples.' It was an essay which he was due to hand in tomorrow. He had no idea what to say. He gazed dully out at the rain, idly noting some boys coming out of the woods.

They must be desperate, he thought, if they have to go out for a smoke in this weather. He returned to his more immediate problem. Who was going to play scrum-half now that Damianos had a sick-chit? He considered the pool of players he could draw on: asthmatics, fatsos, spastics every one. To hell with it. He wrote down Grover's name. They had no chance of winning anyway. He opened his desk cupboard and removed a packet of Jaffa cakes and a large bottle of Coca-Cola. He gulped thirstily from the bottle and ate a few biscuits. *The Rape of the Lock.* What could he say about it? He didn't mind the poem. He thought of Belinda:

'On her white breast a sparkling cross she wore,' . . . He found her far and away the most alluring of the fictional heroines he had yet encountered in his brief acquaintance with English Literature. He read the opening of the poem again. He saw her lying in a huge rumpled bed, a lace peignoir barely covering two breasts as firm and symmetrical as halved grapefruits. He had had a bonk-on all the English lesson. It hadn't happened to him since they'd read *Great Expectations.* What was her name? Estella. God, yes. She was almost as good as Belinda. He thought about his essay again. He liked English Literature. He wondered if he would be able to do it at university – if he could get to university at all. His father had not been at all pleased when he had announced that he wanted to do

English A-level. 'What's the use of that?' he had shouted. 'How's English Literature going to help you sell machine tools?' Niles sighed. There was an opening for him in Gerald Niles (Engineering) Ltd. His father knew nothing of his plans for university.

Niles ran his hands through his thick wiry hair and rubbed his eyes. He picked up his pen. 'Alexander Pope,' he wrote, 'was a major poet of the Augustan period. *The Rape of the Lock* was his most celebrated poem.' He sensed it was a bad beginning – uninspired, boring – but sometimes if you started by writing down what you knew, you occasionally got a few ideas. He scanned Canto One. 'Soft bosoms', he saw. Then 'Belinda still her downy pillow prest'. He felt himself quicken. Pope knew what he was doing, all right. The associations: bosom and pillow, prest and breast. Niles shut his eyes. He was weighing Belinda's perfect breasts in his hands, massaging her awake as she lay in her tousled noonday bed. He imagined her hair spread over her face, full lips, heavy sleep-bruised eyes. He imagined a slim forearm raised to ward off Sol's tim'rous ray, Belinda turning on to her back, stretching. Jesus. Would she have hairy armpits? he wondered, swallowing. Did they shave their armpits in the eighteenth century? Would it be like that French woman he'd seen on a campsite near Limoges last summer? In the camp supermarket, wearing only a bikini, reaching up for a tin on a high shelf and exposing a great hank of armpit hair. Niles groaned. He leant forward and rested his head on his open book. 'Belinda,' he whispered, 'Belinda.'

'Everything okay, Quentin?'

He sat up abruptly, banging his knees sharply on the bottom of his desk. It was Bowler, his housemaster, his round bespectacled face peering at him concernedly, his body canted into the study, pipe clenched between his brown teeth. Why couldn't the bastard knock? Niles swore.

'Trying to write an essay, sir,' he said.

'Not that difficult, is it?' Bowler laughed. 'Got the team for the league?'

Niles handed it over. Bowler studied it, puffing on his pipe, frowning. Niles looked at the sour blue smoke gathering on the ceiling. Typical bloody Bowler.

'This the best we can do? Are you sure about Grover at scrum-half? Crucial position, I would have thought.'

'I think he needs to be pressured a bit, sir.'

'Right-ho. You're the boss. See you're down for *Pinafore*.'

'Sorry, sir?'

'*Pinafore*. HMS. The opera. Didn't know you sang, Quentin? Shouldn't have thought it was your line really.'

'Thought I'd give it a go, sir.'

Bowler left and Niles thought about the opera. Holland

had said it was a sure thing with the girls: they only came because they wanted to get off with boys. Niles wondered what they'd be like. Scottish girls from the local grammar school. He'd seen them in town often. Dark blue uniforms, felt hats, long hair, mini-skirts. They all looked older than him – more mature. He experienced a sudden moment of panic. What in God's name would he do? Holland and Panton would be there, everyone would see him. He felt his heart beat with unreasonable speed. It was a kind of proof. There was no chance of lying or evading the issue. It would be all too public.

They gathered in the music room behind the new chapel for the first mixed rehearsal. There had been three weeks of tedious afternoon practices during which some semblance of singing ability had been forcibly extracted from them by the efforts of Prothero, the music master. Now Prothero watched the boys enter with a tired and cynical smile. This was his seventh Gilbert and Sullivan since coming to the school, his third *HMS Pinafore*. Two sets of forms faced each other at one end of the long room. The boys sat down on one set staring at the empty seats opposite as if they were already occupied.

'Now, gentlemen,' Prothero began. 'The ladies will be here soon. I don't propose to lecture you any more on the subject. I count on your innate good manners and sense of decorum.'

Niles, Holland and Panton sat together. Whispered conversations were going on all around. Niles felt his lungs press against his rib cage. The tension was acute, he felt faint with unfamiliar stress. What if not one of them spoke to him? This was dreadful, he thought, and the girls weren't even here. He looked at the fellow members of the chorus. There were some authentic tenors and basses from the school choir but the rest of them were made up of self-appointed lads, frustrates and sexual braggarts. He could sense their crude desire thrumming through the group as if the forms they were sitting on were charged with a low electric current. He looked at the bright-eyed, snouty, expectant faces, heard whispered obscenities and saw the international language of sexual gesticulation being covertly practised as if they were a gathering of randy deaf-mutes. He felt vaguely soiled to be counted among them. Beside him Holland leaned forward and tapped the shoulder of a boy in front.

'Bloody Mobo,' he said quietly and venomously. 'Didn't you get the message? No queers allowed. What are you bloody doing here? It's girls we're singing with. Not lushmen, Mobo, no little lushmen.'

'Frig off, Holland,' the boy said tonelessly. 'I'm in the choir, aren't I?'

'Bloody choir,' Holland repeated, his face ugly with illogical aggression. 'Bloody frigging choir.'

Then the girls came in.

No one had heard the bus from town arriving and the room, to Niles' startled eyes, seemed suddenly to be filled with chattering uniformed females. He heard laughter and giggles, caught flashing glimpses of cheeks and red mouths, hair and knees as the other half of the chorus sat itself down opposite. The boys fired nervous exploratory glances across the two yards of floor between them. Niles studied his score with commendable intensity. He noticed Holland brazenly scrutinizing the girls. Cautiously, Niles raised his eyes and looked over. They seemed very ordinary, was his first reflection. Dark blue blazers, short skirts, some black tights. There was one tall girl with a severe, rather thin face. Her hair was tied up in an elaborate twisted bun and at first he thought she was a mistress, but then he saw her uniform. He scanned the features of the others but their faces refused to register any individuality – he might have been staring at a Chinese football team.

Holland bowed his head.

'Mm-mm. I've seen mine,' he said in a low voice. 'The blonde in front.' He gave a whimper of suppressed desire. Some boys looked round and smiled, complicity springing up instantly, like recognition.

'Right, everybody,' Prothero shouted, banging out a chord on the piano. 'Page twenty-three please.'

'And I'm never ever sick at sea,' Prothero sang.
  'What never?' boomed the chorus of sailors.
  'No, never,' replied Prothero.
  'What *never?*' the chorus sceptically inquired again.
  'Hardly ever,' Prothero admitted.
  'He's hardly ever sick at sea . . .'
  'Fine,' Prothero called. 'Good, that'll do for today. Thank you, ladies. Your bus should be outside. Scores on the end of the piano as you go out, please.'

The bus was late and the girls had to wait for five minutes outside the chapel. Niles took his time finding his coat in the vestibule and when he went outside Holland and Panton were already talking to four girls. 'Niles, Niles,' they shouted as he emerged into the watery sunlight of a February afternoon. 'Over here.' He walked over, the blood pounding in his ears like surf. Holland stood behind a slim blonde girl with moles on her face, Panton by a cheery-looking redhead. Niles approached. One of the two remaining girls was the tall sharp-faced one he'd seen earlier. The other was small with wispy fair hair and spectacles.

'This is Quentin,' Holland said. 'Hero of the rugby field, captain of the squash team. Master flogger extraordinaire.' 35

'Shut up!' Niles exclaimed, appalled at this slander. 'You bastard.'

'What's a flogger?' Holland's girl asked. Panton was doubled up with mirth. The tall girl looked on expressionlessly.

'Never mind,' Holland said. 'Sorry, Quent. Little joke. Now, this is Joyce,' he indicated Panton's girl. 'This is Helen,' pointing to his own. 'And,' he looked at the tall girl, 'Alison? Yes, Alison. And, um . . .'

'Frances,' said the small girl.

Niles had moved round to stand beside Alison. Frances was clearly on her own. She stood undecidedly for a moment before wandering off without a further word.

Holland and Panton had instinctively sensed out the kind of girl they were after. Innuendoes were already being exchanged with a wanton suggestiveness. Niles looked at Alison. She was tall. In her high heels slightly taller than him. She appeared older, in her twenties almost, but the severity of her face was partly an illusion caused by her schoolmarmy bun. Her skirt was not as short as Helen's or Joyce's; it stopped two inches above her knees. Her legs were long and shapely. On the lapel of her blazer were numerous badges: three Robertson's gollies, a small Canadian maple leaf, a yellow square, and a blue rectangular one with 'monitor' written on it in plain silver letters.

She wore a white shirt, and a tie with the smallest knot in it Niles had ever seen.

He had to say something. He cleared his throat. 'Campaign medals?' he said, pointing to the badges. He realized his finger was two inches from her right breast and he snatched his hand away. He thought she gave the thinnest of smiles in response but he couldn't be sure.

'Cold though,' he said, huffing and puffing into his cupped hands.

She rummaged in her blazer pockets. 'Cigarette?' she asked taking out a packet and offering it to him.

Niles was taken aback by this unselfconsciously adult gesture. 'Christ, no,' he said hurriedly. 'I mean, we're not allowed.'

But she was already offering them to Joyce and Helen. Alison took out a box of matches and lit the others' cigarettes. For some reason Niles was impressed by the capable way she did this – she obviously smoked a lot. Meanwhile Holland and Panton aped nicotine starvation. When Joyce and Helen exhaled they chased the clouds of smoke about, beating it into their gaping mouths with their hands as if it were vital oxygen. The girls laughed delightedly.

'What I'd give for a fag,' said Holland through gritted teeth.

'Oh, yeah?' said lissom Helen.

'Now see what you've done,' Niles said to Alison with more accusation in his voice than he'd meant.

Alison laughed briefly.

Niles brushed his teeth, alone at the row of basins. He rinsed his mouth out and went to stand in front of the large mirror by the urinals. He looked at his square face. He rubbed his jaw. He'd need to shave tomorrow. He had to shave every two days now. Somebody shouted 'Virile!' through the washroom door. Niles whirled round but he didn't see who it was. When he turned back to the mirror his face was red.

He thought about Alison. Everything about her was maddeningly indistinct and ambiguous. All he'd heard her say was 'cigarette?' and 'bye'. It wasn't much to build a relationship on. He had an image of the back of her long legs in their tan tights as she'd climbed on to the bus. He wondered what her breasts were like. Her 'soft bosoms'.

He sighed and belted his dressing gown tighter around him. He walked through the quiet empty house towards his dormitory. A junior came padding down the corridor in pyjamas.

'Where are you going, Payne?' Niles said tiredly.

'For a slash, Niles.'

'Where's your bloody slippers and dressing gown then?'

'Oh Niles,' Payne moaned.

'Get back and bloody put them on.'

'Oh God, Niles, *please*, I just want a pee. I'll only be a second.'

'Go on, you little shit,' Niles raised his hand menacingly. Payne turned and ran back up the corridor.

Niles walked on towards his dormitory. It was a small one, only eight beds. He opened the door quietly. It was well past lights out. The long room was quite dark. He closed the door softly behind him.

'Okay, folks,' came a voice. 'Stop flogging, here's Niles.'

'Shut up, Fillery,' Niles said. Fillery was fat and wicked. His mother was an actress who lived in Cannes.

'What's she like then, Niles?' Fillery said.

'Who?'

'Who? The bloody bird of course, that's who. *Pinafore*. What's your one like?'

'Yeah, go on, Niles,' said another voice. 'Tell us, what's she like?'

'Shut up. I'm warning you lot.'

'Come on, Niles,' Fillery said wheedlingly. 'I bet she's all right. I bet you got a good one.'

Niles got into bed. He lay down and put his hands behind his neck. 'She's okay,' he said grudgingly. 'I'm not complaining.' There were soft groans of envy at this. 'Not bad, I suppose,' he went on. 'She's got nice long legs.'

'What's her name?'

'Alison.'

'Oh Alison, Alison.' People tried out the name on their tongues as if it were a foreign word.

'Tits?' Fillery asked.

'You filthy bugger,' Niles said. 'Trust bloody Fillery.' But Niles felt the lie rise unprompted in his throat. 'They're nice if you must know,' he said. 'Average size. Sort of pointy, if you know what I mean.' There was a chorus of groans at this, deep and despairing. Someone jiggled furiously up and down on his bed causing the springs to creak and complain.

'Shut up,' Niles hissed angrily. 'That's your lot. Now get to sleep.'

He saw Alison at the next rehearsal a week later. Already people had paired off, Helen and Joyce making straight for Holland and Panton at the first break.

'Fifteen minutes, ladies and gentlemen,' Prothero called.

Niles wandered over to Alison. Again he was impressed by her mature looks.

'Hi, there,' he said, as casually as he could.

'Oh . . . hello.' She smiled. 'It's, um, Quentin, isn't it?'

Niles hated his name. ''Fraid so,' he said.

'Phew,' she said. 'Any chance of us having a quiet smoke somewhere?'

They picked their way through the small wood at the back of the chapel. It had rained heavily that morning and the stark trunks of the beech and ash trees were wet and shiny. Alison puffed aggressively at her cigarette. Niles had declined again. He turned up the collar of his blazer and remarked on the inclemency of the season. Alison looked suspiciously at him, as if he were making a joke. Her hair was mid-brown and her skin was very white. She had a thin mouth but her lips were well formed, there was a deep and pronounced dip to her cupid's bow. Niles found this detail endearing, as if somehow this validated his choice of her. His heart seemed to swell with emotion. Their elbows touched as the path narrowed. Niles checked his watch.

'Better not go too far,' he said, then paused before adding, 'they might get suspicious . . .'

'Sure,' Alison said, flicking her cigarette away. 'Smoking like a chimney. I've got Highers in a few months.'

'Mmmm,' Niles sympathized. 'I've got my A's,' he said. 'Then Oxbridge.'

'Are you going to Oxford?' Alison asked. She had a mild Scottish accent, she pronounced the 'r' in Oxford.

'Yes,' he said. 'Well, that's the general idea.' He wondered why he'd lied.

'I'm going to Aberdeen,' she said.

'Ah.'

They walked slowly back to the music room. They were the last to arrive. Holland and Panton looked up admiringly at him as he regained his seat.

'Quent,' Holland whispered. 'You bloody sex-maniac.'

'Shagger,' Panton accused. 'Bloody old shagger, Quent.'

'Quiet please,' Prothero called. 'If you're quite ready, Niles. Now can we have the ensemble? Jolly tars, female relatives and Josephine: "Oh joy oh rapture unforeseen, for now the sky is all serene," right? Two, three.'

'What happened next?' Fillery prompted.

Niles lay in bed. He could sense the entire dormitory waiting in quiet expectancy. Hands on their cocks, he thought.

'We went round the back of the chapel,' he continued. 'Walked into the wood a bit. We sat down on a log. Chatted a bit . . . I could feel the atmosphere between us just building up. We were talking about work, but not talking about it, if you know what I mean. It was more just something to say.'

'Who made the first move?' Fillery asked.

'I did, of course. I was talking. Then I stopped, and looked up. She was looking at me . . . in that sort of way.'

42   'Oh, God.'

'She was looking at me, as if to say . . . and we just sort of moved close together and kissed.'

There was a pause.

'Get your tongue down?'

'*Jesus*, Fillery. One-track bloody mind . . . Yeah, yeah, if you must know every detail. Not at first – the third or fourth kiss. But it got pretty passionate. Frenching just about all the time.'

'Stop it! Stop it!' somebody called. 'I can't stand it any more.'

'What else happened,' Fillery implored. 'Did you . . . you know?'

'We kissed mainly. Hell, we didn't have much time. She was just sort of running her hand through my hair. I got a bit of a feel but not much. I'll have to wait until next week.'

Fillery was quiet. 'God, you bastard, Niles,' he said. 'You lucky bastard.'

On Saturday, after lunch, Holland and Panton bicycled the three miles to the coast. Helen's family kept a caravan on the caravan site by the beach. Helen and Joyce had arranged to meet the boys there. Niles was playing in a first XV rugby match. He heard all about their exploits later in the afternoon. He was in his study changing out of his rugby kit – the school had lost and he thought he'd pulled a muscle in his thigh – when Holland and Panton burst in.

'Oh, my God, Quent,' Holland crowed. 'I don't believe it. It was incredible. They had booze too. I'm pissed.' He held up his middle finger. 'Sticky finger, Quent. First time.'

Niles plucked at his laces. An irrational hatred and resentment for Holland and Panton festered inside him. Holland he didn't mind. Pete was screwing all the time by all accounts. But Panton? He was short-arsed and had spots. Why should he have any luck?

'Get your rocks off then?' he asked without looking up.

'Not this time. They wouldn't let us. But, my God, Nilo, we could, you know, we could. We've got to fix something up.'

Niles felt a vast relief. Just feel-ups then. Big bloody deal.

'Here,' Holland said. 'Almost forgot. A message from Alison. Wey-hey!' With a flourish he handed over a lilac envelope. Niles felt his throat contract. He opened it carefully.

'Any clippings?' Holland asked with a snigger.

'Hardly,' Niles said. Holland had a French girlfriend who used to send him cuttings of her pubic hair. They were cherished and passed round like sacred relics. This fact had single-handedly boosted Holland's reputation to near-legendary heights.

'Dear Quentin,' Niles read. 'I was wondering if by any chance you would like to come and have tea tomorrow

(Sunday). I realize this is short notice but if I don't hear from you I'll expect you at four. I hope you can make it. Sincerely, Alison.'

Niles felt his pulled muscle twitch spasmodically in his thigh. 'I hope you can make it.' That was good. But 'sincerely'? Really!

'What is it, for Christ's sake?' Panton asked.

'Tea,' Niles said. 'Tomorrow afternoon.'

Holland shook his head admiringly. 'You got it made, Quent boy. You are home and dry ... We must get something fixed up though. For all of us. After the last performance maybe. Jesus, the bloody show's over in a couple of weeks.'

Alison's house was a grey sandstone bungalow at the better end of the small Scottish county town near the school. Niles cycled the six miles there through a fine rainy mist and arrived damp and chilled. He met Alison's parents – Mr and Mrs McCullen – and her fourteen-year-old sister Diane. They sat in a warm immaculate sitting room and ate scones and pancakes. The family were kind and genial and Niles relaxed almost immediately and made them laugh with anecdotes of school life. He was a great success with Diane. Alison sat quietly for most of the time, occasionally passing round plates or pouring out more tea. She was wearing jeans and a tight pale blue   45 sweater that gave her a firm breasty look. It was the first time he'd seen her out of uniform and the first time he'd seen her with her hair down. It was long and wavy, dull and thick. It made her look less severe. He felt buoyant with lust and desire, as if he were over-inflated, as if his lungs were crammed with extra capacity of air. He had a sherry before remounting his bike for the long ride back. He reached the school in time for supper.

'I undressed her very slowly,' he told the dormitory. 'As if she was, sort of fragile, or very weak. I unfastened her bra and I kissed her breasts gently. Then . . . then I pulled down her pants and I told her to stand there while I looked at her. She was very slim. Her breasts were firm with almost perfectly round nipples . . .' He swallowed, gazing up unblinkingly at the ceiling as he elaborated his fiction. Even Fillery was silent. 'Then I undressed and we got into bed. I ran my hands all over her body. I wanted to make love but, well, we couldn't because I . . . I didn't have a johnny.'

'I've got dozens,' Fillery said. 'If you'd only asked me.'

'How was I meant to know it would happen?' Niles protested. 'That her parents weren't going to be in? I thought it was just an invitation for tea, for God's sake.'

Niles, Holland and Panton stood at the back of the assembly hall. They were wearing cadet force naval bell-bottoms rolled up to mid calf, singlets and red-spotted neckerchiefs. In front of the stage Prothero was trying to get the school orchestra into tune. On stage Mr Mulcaster, the art teacher, was applying final touches to his backdrop depicting the poop deck of HMS *Pinafore*. Mulcaster's initials were T. A. M., Thomas Anthony Mulcaster. He was known as Tampax Tony.

'Christ Almighty, look at Tampax,' Panton said scornfully. 'It's pathetic. I think he's actually painting in a seagull.'

'Ah, now that's an original touch,' Holland confessed. 'Almost as good as his rigging and halliards.'

'A seagull,' Niles said. 'What's it supposed to be doing? Hovering in one spot for the entire course of the play?'

'Oh, no. He's painting in a ship on the horizon. A three-master me hearties, ar.'

'We've got to work something out,' Holland said seriously. 'We must have something arranged for after the cast party. Think of something for Christ's sake.'

'I've already told you,' Panton said. 'It's got to be the squash courts. They're ideal.'

'Not a chance, mate,' Niles said. 'Do you know what would happen to me if we got caught?'

'Yes. You'd lose your squash colours,' Panton said with heavy sarcasm.

'Jesus, Nilo,' Holland pleaded. 'You're captain of squash. You've got the keys. We can lock the doors behind us. No one'll know.'

'It's all very well for you. I'll get the bloody boot.'

'Come on, Quentin. Think of the orgy we can have. I've got blankets, booze. Look, I promised the girls we'd have a party. They're expecting one. We haven't got much time. It'll all be over after Saturday night. Gone. Finished.'

Niles was pondering Holland's use of the word 'orgy'.

'Okay,' he said. 'I'll think about it. But I'm not promising anything, mind.'

Alison wore a long flouncy dress, that looked as if it were made out of mattress ticking, and a bonnet. Niles stood beside her in the wings. He could hear the audience taking their seats.

'Like the costume,' he said. 'Nervous?'

Alison cocked her head. 'No, I don't think I am, actually.' Niles looked more closely at her. She grew daily more inscrutable. They had seen more of each other during the final run-up to the play but he felt that the bizarre intimacy of their first encounter had never been approached. The prospect of inviting her to the party seemed an awesome task.

48   'Listen,' he began. 'Some of us are having a little "do"

after the cast party on Saturday night. Wondered if you'd fancy coming. You know, select little gathering.'

'Saturday night? After the cast party? Yes, okay.'

'And I want you lot to think about me this time tomorrow night,' Niles told his cowed and quiescent dormitory, 'because,' he paused, exultation setting up a tremor in his voice, 'because this time tomorrow night I shall be making love. Got that? Making love to a real girl.'

Niles gazed transfixed across the stage at Alison. The final performance of *HMS Pinafore* was almost over. Mr Booth, the physics master, as Captain Corcoran, sang to Buttercup – a pre-pubescent boy called Martin – that wherever she might go he would never be untrue to her.

'What, never?' Niles and Alison and the company wanted to know.

'No, never,' asserted Captain Corcoran.

'What . . . *never*?' the cast repeated.

'Well . . .' ad-libbed the Captain. 'Hardly ever.'

'Hardly ever be untrue to thee-ee-ee . . .' the cast echoed at full volume.

'I mean, be honest,' Holland said to assorted members of the cast. 'It's pretty bloody really. I mean, how these people turn up year in year out and pay good money to see that crap I'll never know.' He ate some more of his 49 cream bun and put his arm round Helen. 'Ah, Quentin old son,' he said as Niles came into the dressing room with a paper cup of Coke for Alison. 'A word in your ear.' Niles came over. 'I think we can make our move now. Discreetly though. See you outside the squash courts in five minutes.'

'Be careful,' Niles said to Alison. He held her arm supportively. 'Watch out for these paving stones.' Alison's high heels seemed to ring out with unpropitious clarity as they walked across the courtyard to the squash courts. It was cold and dark and their breath hung in the air long enough for them to walk through the thin clouds before they dispersed. Alison's hair was down and Niles thought she had never looked so beautiful. Her proximity to him and the thought of what was waiting suddenly seemed to make the simple act of walking hideously complicated. He felt as if a sob were lodged in the back of his throat ready to spring from his mouth at any moment.

'I'm okay,' Alison said, and he released her arm.

Holland and Panton were already there with Helen and Joyce.

'At last,' Holland said. 'What've you two been up to? Couldn't wait, eh?' Everyone giggled. Niles bent his head more than he needed to unlock the door into the squash

courts.

Inside number three court they spread rugs on the boards and sat in a circle round a solitary candle placed in a jam jar. Holland unpacked the picnic. There was some Gouda and Ryvita, a piece of Stilton, slices of salami, gherkins and two long, knobbled Polish sausages. From his coat pockets Panton produced a bottle of South African sherry and half a bottle of gin. Paper cups were distributed and the drinks passed around.

Niles drank some neat gin. 'To Gilbert and Sullivan,' he toasted the company.

'Ssh,' Holland said. 'Keep it down, Quentin. Your voice I mean.' There were sniggers at this. Niles didn't dare look at Alison's shadowy face.

They ate their meal with a certain urgent decorum, conscious of the fact that it had to be got out of the way – but in no unseemly rush – before the night's real business could commence. Eventually, after a pre-arranged nod from Holland, Panton said, 'Quiet. I think I can hear someone outside.' Then he leant forward and blew out the candle. This act was followed by a muffled squeal from Joyce and a flurry of whispered instructions, scuffles and collisions as Holland and Panton, Joyce and Helen, gathered up rugs and paper cups and groped their way out of the door to their respective squash courts, leaving number three to Alison and Niles.

Niles sat in a darkness so total it seemed solid and 51

shifting, like deep water. He realized he was holding his breath and let it out slowly. He peered intensely in front of him, a screen of blasting mental supernova and arcing tracer bullets exploding before his eyes, brightening the absence of vision. Only the unyielding firmness of the court floor beneath his buttocks anchored him to the dimensional world.

He heard Alison move. How close was she?

'Are you all right?' he whispered. He stretched out his hand, encountering nothing.

'Yes,' she said. 'Is there anyone?'

'I don't think so. False alarm. Just Panton panicking.' His hand touched her shoulder. 'Sorry. Can't see a thing.'

'I'm here.'

'Oh.' The darkness began to retreat. He sensed rather than saw Alison. He moved across the rug, closer to her.

'Bloody dark.'

'Yes.'

He moved his head towards hers, gently, almost blindly, like two docking space craft. After some soft bumps and readjustments their lips connected tenuously, then sealed. Niles felt his heart swell to inflate his chest as he felt her thin cool lips beneath his. This was the fifth girl he had kissed properly. It remained as thrilling and exciting as the first time. He wondered if he would always feel this way. With little grunts and discreet pressures he managed to lie Alison down on the rug. Her long hair caught across his face, strands filling his mouth which he had to pull free with his fingers. They kissed again. Niles felt enormously humble and reverential. The accumulated sensations of triumph and release in a kiss were almost enough for him really, but he promptly banished such heretical thoughts from his mind. He managed to get both his arms round Alison and he felt her hands move on his back. His head was resting comfortably on his own left shoulder, Alison's head nestled in the crook of his left elbow. Their knees were touching, her face was perhaps three inches away from his. Some faint source of light picked out a curve on a cheekbone, a glimmer in an eye. The warm breath of her exhalations grazed his cheek. What should he do now, he wondered? Had he much time? What would she like him to do? What was she expecting? Perhaps she wanted to make love too? The novelty of this last idea came to him as rather a shock. He felt suddenly vulnerable and insecure: he sensed the alien presence of her femininity descend on and enfold him. He became immediately aware of his vast ignorance about Alison – the person, the girl – separating him ineluctably from her. Despite the fact that they were lying in each other's arms they might have been facing each other across some great river estuary. The figure on the far bank was a girl's, yes, but that was all he knew.

He felt a gentle shaking. He woke up with a start. His eyes were open but he saw nothing. He sat up. His left arm was dead. It flopped lifelessly at his side.

'You've been asleep,' Alison said. 'I've got to go.'

'What?'

'It's just gone eleven. I've got to get the last bus.'

'Jesus. Asleep? You mean I . . . How long was . . .?'

'You just drifted off. You've been sleeping about half an hour. I didn't want to wake you.'

Niles felt shame and disgrace cause tears to prickle at the corner of his eyes. He picked up his left hand and started to massage it. In the darkness it was like holding an amputated limb. To his right hand his nerveless left felt rough and calloused, like a stranger's.

'Can you find the door?'

They went outside. Alison wondered about the remains of the picnic. Niles told her he'd clean up in the morning before anyone came.

He was about to lock the door. 'What about the others?' he asked, fighting to keep the bitterness from his voice.

'They left about ten minutes ago. I heard them going.'

Niles locked the squash court door. He gazed bleakly around him. Alison stood patiently, knotting her scarf at her throat. It was a sharp, frosty night. The school buildings loomed on either side, dark and unpeopled.

54   'I'd better go, Quentin,' Alison said.

'I'll come with you to the bus stop.'

They set out together, Niles looking nervously back over his shoulder. He was taking a calculated risk. The bus stop lay half a mile beyond the school gates. If he was caught out of bounds with a girl at this time of night he would be in serious trouble. But equally he felt that whatever happened nothing should prevent him from being with Alison at this moment. They walked on in silence. Niles' mind was a tangle of conflicting emotions. Sentences formed in his head only to split into whirling separate words like some modish animated film. He felt he should say something, explain that he hadn't meant to fall asleep, allude to his romantic plans, but his tongue and his mind refused to co-ordinate. His brain seemed to lock into an imbecilic stupidity. He couldn't do anything right.

At the school gates he let Alison stride confidently through and go a little way down the road before he snaked beneath the lodge windows, squirmed through the side gate and made a sequence of zig-zag dashes from bush to tree trunk, like a commando behind enemy lines, before he caught up with her.

Alison stood in the middle of the road waiting for him. 'That's a bit dramatic, isn't it?'

'I'm out of bounds, you see. If I get caught . . .'

'I don't want you to get into trouble, Quentin.'

'Forget it, really. I don't care.' He took her hand. 55

There was a small shelter by the bus stop . . . 'Come on, let's go.' They walked briskly down the road.

The shelter was empty. A nearby street light threw the graffiti carved on its green wooden bench into high relief. Small drifts of cigarette packs, soft drink cans and wrappers were banked beneath it.

'Alison,' Niles began. 'Listen. I have to say this, I don't want you to think that . . .'

'Here it comes,' cried Alison, as the bus appeared round the corner. 'That was lucky.'

The bus stopped. She gave him a swift kiss on the cheek, so swift it was almost a clash of heads, and got on. Niles looked at the single decker bus. Inside it was soft yellow and smoky. A couple of old women looked curiously back at him. On the rear seats some louts drank beer from cans. Alison stood at the top of the steps, her back to him, buying her ticket from the driver. Her long legs seemed twin symbols of rebuke.

'I'll phone,' he shouted, louder than he meant. It sounded like a grievance, a threat. She turned, smiled, and walked down the bus to take her seat. Niles saw her thick dark hair on her blazer, saw her head toss as she sat down. She waved. The bus drove off. He didn't wave back.

Niles walked morosely up the drive. He walked on the verge, ready to duck behind one of the beech trees that lined the road should a car come by. He stumbled over a root, stopped, turned and kicked savagely at it. In a sombre mood of reassessment he cursed his school, the closed society he was compelled to live in, his demanding, predatory, so-called friends. 'Women,' his father had once patronizingly told him, 'are a lifetime's study.' He was off to a late start then, he observed grimly, and wondered if he would ever catch up. He felt suddenly exhausted by the daily, monotonous absorption with sex, disgusted by the lonely idolatry of masturbation. He felt that his sexual nature, whatever it might be, was irretrievably corrupted.

He paused and took a few deep breaths, trying to shake the mood from him. At this point the drive curved gently to the right, back towards main school. On his left and ahead of him lay a wide flat expanse of playing fields, fixed and still under a faint starlight. His house lay in that direction. It would be quicker, but he wondered if he dared expose himself on the open space. He made up his mind. He set off, breaking into a steady jog, feeling the frost cracking under his feet, puffing his condensed breath ahead of him like a steam engine. He loped silently and strongly across the pitches. He felt that he could run for ever. He would be back in the dorm before twelve. They would all be waiting for him. Fillery had said they'd stay up specially. They wanted to know everything, Fillery had said, every little detail. The bastards, Niles said to himself, smiling. His mind began to work. He'd give them a good story tonight, all right. They wouldn't forget this one in a long time. He ran on, a strange jubilation lengthening his stride.

Gifts

We land in Nice. Pan Am. I go through customs without much trouble and stand around the arrivals hall wondering what to do next – if there's a bus into town; whether I should get a taxi. I see a man – black hair, white face, blue suit – looking curiously at me. I decide to ignore him.

He comes over, though.

'Tupperware?' he asks unctuously. He pronounces it tooperwère.

'Sorry?' I say.

'Ah, English,' he says with some satisfaction, as if he's done something clever. 'Mr Simpson.' He picks up my suitcase, it's heavier than he expects. He has tinted spectacles and his black hair is getting thin at the front. He looks about forty.

'No,' I say. I tell him my name.

He puts my suitcase down. He looks around the arrivals hall at the few remaining passengers. I am the only one not being met.

'*Merde*,' he swears softly. He shrugs his shoulders. 'Do you want a ride into town?'

We go outside to his car. It's a big Citroën. The back is

filled with plastic beakers, freezer boxes, salad crispers and such like. He puts my case in the boot. He shovels stacks of pamphlets off the front seat before he lets me into his car. He explains that he has been sent to meet his English opposite number from Tupperware UK. He says he assumed I was English from my clothes. In fact, he goes on to claim that he can guess any European's nationality from the kind of clothes he or she is wearing. I ask him if he can distinguish Norwegians from Danes and for some reason he seems to find this very funny.

We drive off smartly, following the signs for Nice *centre ville*. I can't think of anything to say as my French isn't good enough and somehow I don't like the idea of talking to this man in English. He sits very close to the steering wheel and whistles softly through his teeth, occasionally raising one hand in rebuke at any car that cuts in too abruptly on him. He asks me, in French, how old I am and I tell him I'm eighteen. He says I look older than that.

After a while he reaches into the glove compartment and takes out some photographs. He passes them over to me.

'You like?' he says in English.

They are pictures of him on a beach standing by some rocks. He is absolutely naked. He looks in good shape for a forty-year-old man. In one picture I see he's squatting down and some trick of the sun and shadow makes his cock seem enormously long.

'Very nice,' I say, handing them back, 'but *non merci*.'

He drops me in the middle of the Promenade des Anglais. We shake hands and he drives off. I stand for a while looking down on the small strip of pebble beach. It's January and the beach is empty. The sky is packed with grey clouds and the sea looks an unpleasant blue-green. For some reason I was expecting sunshine and parasols. I let my eyes follow the gentle curve of the Baie des Anges. I start at the airport and travel along the sweep of the coast. The palm trees, the neat little Los Angeleno-style hotels with their clipped poplars and fancy wrought iron-work, along past the first of the apartment blocks, blind and drab with their shutters firmly down, past the Negresco with its pink sugary domes, past the Palais de la Méditérranée, along over the old Port, completing the slow arc at the promontory of Cap St Jean, surmounted by its impossible villa. I see the ferry from Corsica steaming gamely into harbour. I stand looking for a while until I begin to feel a bit cold.

It's Sunday so I can't enrol for my courses at the university until the next day. I carry my case across the Promenade des Anglais, go up one street and book into the first hotel

I see. It's called the Hotel Astoria. I go down some steps into a dim foyer. An old man gives me a room.

I sit in my room reading for most of the evening. At about half past nine I go out for a coffee. Coming back to the hotel I notice several young girls standing in front of brightly lit shop windows in the Rue de France. Despite the time of year they are wearing boots and hot pants. They all carry umbrellas (unopened) and swing bunches of keys. I walk past them two or three times but they don't pay much attention. I observe that some of them are astoundingly pretty. Every now and then a car stops, there is a brief conversation, one of the girls gets in and is driven away.

Later that night as I am sitting on my bed reading there is a knock on my door. It turns out to be the fat daughter of the hotel manager. He has told her I am English and she asks if I will help her do a translation that she's been set for homework.

I enrol at the university. This takes place at a building called the Centre Universitaire Méditérranéan or CUM as it's generally known (the French pronounce it 'cume'). The building is on the Promenade des Anglais and looks like a small, exclusive art gallery. Inside there is a huge lecture room with a dull mythological mural on three walls. This morning I am the first to arrive and there is a hushed marmoreal stillness in the place. In a small office I enrol and pay my fees. I decide to postpone my first class until the next day as I have to find somewhere to live. A secretary gives me a list of addresses where I can rent a room. I look for the cheapest. Mme D'Amico, it says at the bottom of the list, 4 Rue Dante. I like the address.

As I leave the Centre I see some of my fellow students for the first time. They all seem to be foreign – in the sense that not many are French. I notice a tall American girl surrounded by chattering Nigerians. There are some Arabs. Some very blonde girls whom I take to be Scandinavian. Soon the capacious marble-floored entrance hall begins to fill up as more and more people arrive for their classes. I hear the pop-pop of a motor bike in the small courtyard at the front. Two young guys with long hair come in talking English. Everyone seems happy and friendly. I leave.

Rue Dante is not far from the Centre. Number four is a tall old apartment block with bleached shutters and crumbling stone work. On the ground floor is a café. CAVE DANTE it says in plastic letters. I ask the concierge for Mme D'Amico and am directed up three flights of stairs to the top floor. I ring the bell, mentally running through the phrases I have prepared. '*Mme D'Amico? Je suis étudiant anglais. Je cherche une chambre. On m'a donné votre nom au Centre Universitaire Méditérranéan.*' I ring the bell again and hear vague stirrings from the flat. I sense I am being stared at through the peep-hole set in the solid wooden door. After a lengthy time of appraisal, it opens.

Mme D'Amico is very small – well under five feet. She has a pale, thin, wrinkled face and grey hair. She is dressed in black. On her feet she is wearing carpet slippers which seem preposterously large, more suitable for a thirteen-stone man. I learn later that this is because sometimes her feet swell up like balloons. Her eyes are brown and, though a little rheumy, are bright with candid suspicion. However, she seems to understand my French and asks me to come in.

Her flat is unnervingly dark. This is because use of the electric lights is forbidden during hours of daylight. We stand in a long gloomy hallway off which several doors lead. I sense shapes – a wardrobe, a hatstand, a chest, even what I take to be a gas cooker, but I assume my eyes are not yet accustomed to the murk. Mme D'Amico shows me into the first room on the left. She opens shutters. I see a bed, a table, a chair, a wardrobe. The floor is made of loose red hexagonal tiles that click beneath my feet as I walk across to look out of the window. I peer down into the apartment building's central courtyard. Far below the concierge's Alsatian is scratching itself. From my window

I can see into at least five other apartments. I decide to stay here.

Turning round I observe the room's smaller details. The table is covered with a red and brown checked oilcloth on which sits a tin ashtray with 'SUZE' printed on it. On one wall Mme D'Amico has affixed two posters. One is of Mont Blanc. The other is an SNCF poster of Biarritz. The sun has faded all the bright colours to grey and blue. Biarritz looks as cold and unwelcoming as the Alps.

I am not the only lodger at Mme D'Amico's. There is a muscle-bound taciturn engineer called Hugues. His room is separated from mine by the WC. He is married and goes home every weekend to his wife and family in Grenoble. Two days after I arrive the phone rings while I am alone in the flat. It is Hugues' wife and she sounds nervous and excited. I somehow manage to inform her that Hugues is out. After some moments of incomprehension I eventually gather that it is imperative for Hugues to phone her when he comes in. I say I will give him the message. I sweat blood over that message. I get my grammar book and dictionary out and go through at least a dozen drafts. Finally I prop it by the phone. It was worth the effort. Hugues is very grateful and from that day more forthcoming, and Mme D'Amico makes a point of congratulating me on my French. She seems more impressed by my error-free and correctly accented prose than by anything else about me. So much so that she asks me if I want to watch TV with her tonight. I sense that this is something of a breakthrough: Hugues doesn't watch her TV. But then maybe he has better things to do.

Almost without any exertion on my part, my days take on a pattern. I go to the Centre in the morning and afternoon for my courses. At lunch and in the evening I eat at the enormous university cafeteria up by the Law faculty. I return home, have a cup of coffee in the Cave Dante, then pass the rest of the evening watching TV with Mme D'Amico and a neighbour – a fat jolly woman to whom I have never been introduced but whose name, I know, is Mme Franchot.

Mme D'Amico and Mme Franchot sit in armchairs. I bring a wooden chair in from the hall and sit behind them looking at the screen between their heads. While the TV is on all other source of illumination is switched off and we sit and watch in a spectral grey light. Mme D'Amico reads out loud every piece of writing that appears on the screen – the titles of programmes, the entire list of credits, the names and endorsements of products being advertised. At first I find this intensely irritating and the persistent commentary almost insupportable. But she speaks fairly softly and after a while I get used to her voice.

We watch TV in Mme D'Amico's bedroom. She has no sitting room as such. I think that used to be the function of my room. Hugues sleeps in what was the kitchen. He has a sink unit at the foot of his bed. Mme D'Amico cooks in the hall (I was right: it was a cooker) and washes up in the tiny bathroom. This contains only a basin and a bidet and there are knives and forks laid out alongside toothbrushes and flannels on a glass shelf. There is no bath, which proved something of a problem to me at the outset as I'm quite a clean person. So every two or three days I go to the municipal swimming baths at the Place Magnan. Formal, cheerless, cold, with pale green tiles everywhere, but it stops me from smelling.

The fourth room in the flat is a dining room, though it's never used for this purpose as this is where Mme D'Amico works. She works for her son, who is something – a shipper I think – in the wine trade. Her job is to attach string to a label illustrating the region the wine comes from and then to tie the completed label round the neck of a wine bottle. The room is piled high with crates of wine, which she sometimes calls on me to shift. Most days when I come back I see her sitting there, patiently tying labels round the necks of the wine bottles. It must be an incredibly boring job. I've no idea how much her son pays her but I suspect it's very little. But Mme D'Amico is methodical and busy. She works like hell. People are always coming to take away the completed crates. I like to think she's really stinging her son.

There are lots of girls I'd like to fuck who do courses with me at the Centre. Lots. I sit there in the class with them and think about it, unable to concentrate on my studies. I've spoken to a few people but I can't as yet call any of them friends. I know a Spanish girl and an English girl but they both live outside Nice with their parents. The English girl is called Victoria and is chased all day by a Tunisian called Rida. Victoria's father was a group captain in the RAF and has retired to live in Grasse. 'Out to Grasse' Victoria calls it. Somehow I don't think the group captain would like Rida. Victoria is a small, bland blonde. Not very attractive at all, but Rida is determined. You've got to admire his persistence. He doesn't try anything on, is just courteous and helpful, tries to make Victoria laugh. He never leaves her side all day. I'm sure if he perseveres his luck will turn. Victoria seems untroubled by his constant presence, but I can't see anything in Rida that would make him attractive to a girl. He is of average height, wears bright-coloured, cheap-looking clothes. His hair has a semi-negroid kink in it which he tries to hide by ruthlessly brushing it flat against his head. But his hair is too long for this style to be effective and it sticks out at the sides and the back like a helmet or an ill-fitting wavy cap.

There are genuine pleasures to be derived from having a room of one's own. Sometimes at night I fling back the covers and masturbate dreamily about the girls at the Centre. There is a Swedish girl called Danni whom I like very much. She has big breasts and long white-blonde hair. Is very laughing and friendly. The only trouble is that one of her legs is considerably thinner than the other. I believe she had polio when young. I think about going to bed with her and wonder if this defect would put me off.

My relationship with Mme D'Amico is very formal and correct. We converse in polite phrases that would not disgrace a Victorian drawing room. She asks me, one day, to fill out a white *fiche* for the police – something, she assures me hastily, every resident must do. She notices my age on the card and raises her eyebrows in mild surprise. She says she hadn't supposed me to be so young. Then one morning, *à propos* of nothing, she explains why she reads everything that appears on TV. It seems that Mme Franchot is illiterate. If Mme D'Amico didn't relate them to her, she would never even know the names of the old 69 films we watch nightly on Monte Carlo TV. I find I am surprisingly touched by this confidence.

One evening I go to a café with Rida after our courses and meet up with some of his Tunisian friends. They are all enrolled at one educational institution or another for the sake of the *carte d'étudiant*. They tell me it's very valuable, that they would not be allowed to stay in France if they didn't possess one. Rida, it has to be said, is one of the few who actually tries to learn something. He shares a room with a man called Ali who is very tall and dapper. Ali wears a blazer with brass buttons that has a pseudo-English crest on the breast pocket. Ali says he bought it off a tourist. The English style is *très chic* this year. We drink some beer. Rida tells me how he and Ali recently met a Swiss girl who was hitch-hiking around Europe. They took her back to their room and kept her there. They locked her in during the day. Rida lowers his voice. '*On l'a baissé*,' he tells me conspiratorially. '*Baisser. Tu comprends?*' He says he's sure she was on drugs as she didn't seem to mind, didn't object at all. She escaped one afternoon and stole all their stuff.

The café is small, every shiny surface lined with grease. It gets hot as the evening progresses. There is one very hard-faced blonde woman who works the cash register behind the bar, otherwise we are all men.

I drink too much beer. I watch the Tunisians sodomize the pinball machine, banging and humping their pelvises against the flat end. The four legs squeal their outrage angrily on the tiled floor. At the end of the evening I lend Rida and Ali twenty francs each.

Another phone call when I'm alone in the flat. It's from a doctor. He says to tell Mme D'Amico that it is all right for her to visit her husband on Saturday. I am a little surprised. I never imagined Mme D'Amico had a husband – because she always wears black I suppose. I pass on the message and she explains that her husband lives in a sanatorium. He has a disease. She starts trembling and twitching all over in graphic illustration.

'Oh,' I say. 'Parkinson's disease.'

'Oui,' she acknowledges. 'C'est ça. Parkingsums.'

This unsought for participation in Mme D'Amico's life removes another barrier. From this day on she uses my first name – always prefixed, however, by 'Monsieur'. 'Monsieur Edward', she calls me. I begin to feel more at home.

I see that it was a misplaced act of generosity on my part to lend Rida and Ali that money as I am now beginning to run short myself. There is a postal strike in Britain which is lasting far longer than I expected. It is quite impossible 71 to get any money out. Foolishly I expected the strike to be short-lived. I calculate that if I radically trim my budget I can last for another three weeks, or perhaps a little longer. Assuming, that is, that Rida and Ali pay me back.

When there is nothing worth watching on television I sit at the window of my room – with the lights off – and watch the life going on in the apartments round the courtyard. I can see Lucien, the *patron* of the Cave Dante, sitting at a table reading a newspaper. Lucien and his wife share their apartment with Lucien's brother and his wife. They all work in the café. Lucien is a gentle bald man with a high voice. His wife has a moustache and old-fashioned, black-framed, almond-shaped spectacles. Lucien's brother is a big hairy fellow called Jean-Louis, who cooks in the café's small kitchen. His wife is a strapping blonde who reminds me vaguely of Simone Signoret. One night she didn't draw the curtains in her bedroom properly and I had quite a good view of her undressing.

I am now running so low on money that I limit myself to one cup of coffee a day. I eat apples all morning and afternoon until it is time for my solitary meal in the university restaurant up by the *fac du droit*. I wait until
72 the end because then they give away free second helpings

of rice and pasta if they have any left over. Often I am the only person in the shining well-lit hall. I sit eating bowl after bowl of rice and pasta while the floors are swabbed around me and I am gradually hemmed in by chairs being set on the tables. After that I wander around the centre of town for a while. At half nine I make my way back to the flat. The whores all come out at half nine precisely. It's quite amazing. Suddenly they're everywhere. Rue Dante, it so happens, is right in the middle of the red-light district. Sometimes on my way back the girls solicit me. I laugh in a carefree manner, shrug my shoulders and tell them I'm an impoverished student. I have this fantasy that one night one of the girls will offer to do it free but so far I've had no success.

If I've saved up my cup of coffee for the evening my day ends at the Cave Dante. I sit up at the zinc bar. Lucien knows my order by now and he sets about making up a *grande crème* as soon as I come in the door. On the top of the bar are baskets for brioches, croissants and pizza. Sometimes there are a few left over from breakfast and lunch. One night I have a handful of spare centimes and I ask Lucien how much the remaining bit of pizza costs. To my embarrassment I still don't have enough to buy it. I mutter something about not being hungry and say I've changed my mind. Lucien looks at me for a moment and tells me to help myself. Now every night I go in and finish off what's left. Each time I feel a flood of maudlin sentiment for the man but he seems uneasy when I try to express my gratitude.

One of the problems about being poor is that I can't afford to send my clothes to the '*Pressings*' any more. And Mme D'Amico won't allow washing in the flat. Dirty shirts mount up on the back of my single chair like so many soiled antimacassars. In a corner of the wardrobe I keep dirty socks and underpants. I occasionally spray the damp heap with my aerosol deodorant as if I were some fastidious pest controller. When all my shirts are dirty I evolve a complicated rota for wearing them. The idea is that I wear them each for one day, trying to allow a week between subsequent wears in the faint hope that the delay will somehow have rendered them cleaner. At least it will take longer for them to get *really* dirty. At the weekend I surreptitiously wash a pair of socks and underpants and sneak them out of the house. I go down to an isolated part of the beach and spread them on the pebbles where a watery February sun does a reasonable job of drying them out.

One Saturday afternoon I am sitting on the shingle beach employed in just such a way. I wonder sadly if this will be my last weekend in Nice. The postal strike wears on, I have forty-two francs and a plane ticket to London. Small breakers nudge and rearrange the pebbles at the water's edge. This afternoon the sea is filled with weed and faeces from an untreated sewage outlet a little way up the coast. Freak tides have swept the effluence into the Baie des Anges. The sun shines, but it is a cool and uncongenial day.

The thought of leaving Nice fills me with an intolerable frustration. Nice has a job to do for me, a function to fulfil and it hasn't even begun to discharge its responsibility.

I hear steps crunching on the stones, coming towards me. I look round. It is Rida with a girl I don't recognize. Frantically I stuff my washing into its plastic bag.

'*Salut*,' Rida says.

'*Ça va?*' I reply nonchalantly.

'What are you doing here?' Rida asks.

'Oh . . . nothing particular.'

We exchange a few words. I look carefully at the girl. She is wearing jeans and a tie-dyed T-shirt. She has reddish-blonde medium-length hair and a flat freckly face. It is not unattractive though. Her eyebrows are plucked away to thin lines and her nose is small and sharp. She seems confident and relaxed. To my surprise Rida tells me she's English.

'English?' I say.

'Hi,' she says. 'My name's Jackie.'

Rida has literally just picked her up on the Promenade. I don't know how he singles them out. I think he feels he has another Swiss girl here. He saw me sitting on the beach and told Jackie he knew an English guy he would like her to meet.

We sit around for a bit. I talk in English to Jackie. We swap backgrounds. She comes from Cheshire and has been living in Nice for the last four months. Latterly she has worked as au pair to a black American family. The father is a professional basketball player, one of several who play in the French leagues now that they're too old or too unfit to make the grade in the US.

With all this English being spoken Rida is beginning to feel left out of it, and is impatiently throwing pebbles into the sea. However, he knows that the only way for him to get this girl is through me and so he suggests we all go to a disco. I like the sound of this because I sense by now that Jackie is not totally indifferent to me herself. She suggests we go to the 'Psyché', a rather exclusive disco on the Promenade des Anglais. I try to disguise my disappointment. The 'Psyché' costs eighteen francs to get in. Then I remember that Rida still owes me twenty francs. I remind him of this fact. I'll go, I say, as long as he pays me in. Reluctantly he agrees.

We meet at nine outside the 'Psyché'. Jackie is wearing

white jeans and a scoop-necked sequinned T-shirt. She has pink shiny lipstick and her hair looks clean and freshly brushed. Rida is wearing black flared trousers and a black lacy see-through shirt unbuttoned down the front. Round his neck he has hung a heavy gold medallion. I'm glad he's changed. As we go in he touches me on the elbow.

'She's mine, okay?' he says, smiling.

'Ah-ha,' I counter. 'I think we should rather leave that up to Jackie, don't you?'

It is my bad luck that Jackie likes to dance what the French call *le Swing* but which the English know as the jive. I find this dance quite impossible to master. Rida, on the other hand, is something of an expert. I sit in a dark rounded alcove with a whisky and coke (a free drink comes with the entry fee) and nervously bide my time.

Rida and Jackie come and sit down. I see small beads of sweat on Jackie's face. Rida's lace shirt is pasted to his back. We talk. A slow record comes on and I ask Jackie to dance. We sway easily to the music. Her body is hot against mine. Her clean hair is dark and damp at her temples. As if it is the most natural thing in the world I rest my lips on the base of her neck. It is damp too, from her recent exertions in *le Swing*. Her hand moves half an inch on my back. I kiss her cheek, then her mouth. She won't use her tongue. She puts her arms round my neck. I break off for a few seconds and glance over at Rida. He is looking at us. He lights a cigarette and scrutinizes its glowing end.

To my astonishment when we sit down Jackie immediately asks Rida if he'd like to dance again as another *Swing* record has come on. She dances with him for a while, Rida spinning her expertly around. I sip my whisky and coke – which is fizzless by now – and wonder what Jackie is up to. She's a curious girl. When they come off the dance floor Rida announces he has to go. We express our disappointment. As he shakes my hand he gives me a wink. No hard feeling, I think he wants to say.

We go, some time later, to another club called le Go-Go. Jackie pays for me to get in. Inside we meet one of Jackie's basketballers. He is very black – almost Nubian in appearance – and unbelievably tall and thin. He is clearly something of a sporting celebrity in Nice, as we get a continuous supply of free drinks while sitting at his table. I drink a lot more whisky and coke. Presently we are joined by three more black basketball players. I become very subdued. The blacks are friendly and extrovert. They wear a lot of very expensive-looking jewelry. Jackie dances with them all, flirts harmlessly, sits on their knees and shrieks with laughter at their jokes. All the French in the club seem to adore them. People keep coming over to our table to ask for autographs. I feel small and anaemic beside them. My personality seems lamentably pretentious and unformed. I think of my poverty, my dirty clothes, my shabby room and I ache with an alien's self-pity, sense a refugee's angst in my bones.

Then Jackie says to me, 'Shall we go?' and suddenly I feel restored. We walk through quiet empty streets, the only sound the rush of water in gutters as they are automatically swilled clean. We pass a café with three tarts inside waiting for their pimp. They chatter away exuberantly.

Jackie shivers and I obligingly put my arm around her. She rests her head on my shoulder and in this fashion we awkwardly make our way to her flat. 'Shh,' Jackie cautions as we open the front door, 'be careful you don't wake them up.' I feel a rising pressure in my throat, and I wonder if the bed has squeaky springs.

We sit in the small kitchen on hard modern chairs. My buttocks feel numb and strangely cold. The fluorescent light, I'm sure, can't be flattering if its unkind effects on Jackie's pale face are anything to go by. Slowly I sense a leaden despair settle on me as we sit in this cheerless efficient module in this expensive apartment block. *Immeuble de très grand standing* the agent's advertisement says outside. We have kissed from time to time and I have felt both her small pointed breasts through her T-shirt. Her lips are thin and provide no soft cushion for my own. We talk now in a listless desultory fashion.

Jackie tells me she's leaving Nice next week to return to England. She wants to be a stewardess she says, but only on domestic flights. Intercontinental ones, it seems, play hell with your complexion and menstrual cycle. Half-heartedly I offer the opinion that it might be amusing if, say, one day I should find myself flying on the very plane in which she was serving. Jackie's face becomes surprisingly animated at this notion. It seems an appropriate time to exchange addresses, which we do. I notice she spells her name 'Jacqui'.

This talk of parting brings with it a small cargo of emotion.

We kiss again and I slip my hand inside her T-shirt.

'No,' she says gently but with redoubtable firmness.

'Please, Jackie,' I say. 'You're going soon.' I suddenly feel very tired. 'Well, at least let me see them then,' I say with petulant audacity. Jackie pauses for a moment, her head cocked to one side as if she can hear someone calling her name in the distance.

'Okay then,' she says. 'If that's what you want. If that's all.'

She stands up, pulls off her T-shirt and slips down the

straps of her bra so that the cups fall free. Her breasts cast no shadow in the unreal glare of the strip-light. The nipples are very small, her breasts are pale and conical and seem almost to point upward. She exposes them for five seconds or so, not looking at me, looking down at her breasts as if she's seeing them for the first time. Then she resnuggles them in her bra and puts her T-shirt back on. She makes no comment at all. It's as if she's been showing me her appendix scar.

'Look,' she says unconcernedly at the door, 'I'll give you a ring before I leave. Perhaps we could get together.'

'Yes,' I say. 'Do. That would be nice.'

Outside it is light. I check my watch. It's half past five. It's cold and the sky is packed with grey clouds. I walk slowly back to Mme D'Amico's through a sharp-focused, scathing dawn light. Some of the cafés are open already. Drowsy *patrons* sweep the pavements. I feel grimy and hungover. I plod up the stairs to Mme D'Amico's. My room, it seems to me, has a distinct fusty, purulent odour; the atmosphere has a stale recycled quality, all the more acute after the uncompromising air of the morning. I strip off my clothes. I add my unnaturally soft shirt to the pile on the back of the chair. I knot my socks and ball my underpants – as if to trap their smells within their folds – and flip them into the corner of the wardrobe. I lie naked 81 between the sheets. Itches start up all over my body. I finger myself experimentally but I'm too tired and too sad to be bothered.

I wake up to a tremulous knocking on my door. I feel dreadful. I squint at my watch. It's seven o'clock. I can't have been asleep for more than an hour.

'*Monsieur Edward? C'est moi, Madame D'Amico.*'

I say come in, but no sound issues from my mouth. I cough and run my tongue over my teeth, swallowing energetically.

'*Entrez, Madame,*' I whisper.

Mme D'Amico comes in. Her hair is pinned up carelessly and her old face is shiny with tears. She sits down on the bed and immediately begins to sob quietly, her thin shoulders shaking beneath her black cardigan.

'Oh, Madame,' I say, alarmed. 'What is it?' I find it distressing to see Mme D'Amico, normally so correct and so formal, displaying such unabashed human weakness. I am also – inappropriately – very aware of my nakedness beneath the sheets.

'*C'est mon mari,*' she cries. '*Il est mort.*'

Gradually the story comes out. Apparently Monsieur D'Amico, sufferer from Parkinson's disease, was having a final cigarette in his room in the sanatorium before the nurse came to put him to bed. He lit his cigarette and then tried to shake the match out. But his affliction instead made the match spin from his trembling fingers and fall down the side of the plastic armchair upon which he was sitting. The chair was blazing within seconds, Monsieur D'Amico's pyjamas and dressing gown caught fire and although he managed to wriggle himself on to the floor his screams were not sufficiently loud to attract the attention of the nurses immediately. He was severely burned. The shock was too much for his frail body and he died in the early hours of the morning.

I try to arrange my sleepy unresponsive senses into some sort of order, try to summon the full extent of my French vocabulary.

Mme D'Amico looks at me pitifully. '*Oh, Monsieur Edward,*' she whimpers, her lips quivering.

'*Madame,*' I reply helplessly. '*C'est une vraie tragédie.*' It seems grossly inept, under the circumstances, almost flippant, my thick early-morning tongue removing any vestige of sincerity from the words. But it seems to mean something to Mme D'Amico, who bows her head and starts to cry with light high-pitched sobs. I reach out an arm from beneath the sheets and gently pat her shoulder.

'There, there, Madame,' I say. 'It will be all right.'

As I lean forward I notice that in her hands there is a crumpled letter. Peering closer I still can't make out the name but I do see that the stamp is British. It is surely for me. The postal strike, I realize with a start, must now be over. Suddenly I know that I can stay. I think at once about Jackie and our bizarre and unsatisfactory evening. But I don't really care any more. My spirits begin to stir and lift. I get a brief mental flash of Monsieur D'Amico in his blazing armchair and I hear the quiet sobs of his wife beside me. But it doesn't really impede the revelation that slowly overtakes me. People, it seems, want to give me things – for some reason known only to them. No matter what I do or how I behave, unprompted and unsought the gifts come. And they will keep on coming. Naked photos, cold pizza, their girls, their wives, their breasts to see, even their grief. I feel a growing confidence about my stay in Nice. It will be all right now, I feel sure. It will work out. I think about all the gifts that lie waiting for me. I think about the Swedish girls at the Centre. I think about spring and the days when the sun will be out . . .

The bed continues to shudder gently from Mme D'Amico's sobbing. I smile benignly at her bowed head.

'There, there, Madame,' I say again. 'Don't worry. Everything will be okay. You'll see. Everything will be fine, I promise you.'

PENGUIN 60s

MARTIN AMIS · *God's Dice*
HANS CHRISTIAN ANDERSEN · *The Emperor's New Clothes*
MARCUS AURELIUS · *Meditations*
JAMES BALDWIN · *Sonny's Blues*
AMBROSE BIERCE · *An Occurrence at Owl Creek Bridge*
DIRK BOGARDE · *From Le Pigeonnier*
WILLIAM BOYD · *Killing Lizards*
POPPY Z. BRITE · *His Mouth will Taste of Wormwood*
ITALO CALVINO · *Ten Italian Folktales*
ALBERT CAMUS · *Summer*
TRUMAN CAPOTE · *First and Last*
RAYMOND CHANDLER · *Goldfish*
ANTON CHEKHOV · *The Black Monk*
ROALD DAHL · *Lamb to the Slaughter*
ELIZABETH DAVID · *I'll be with You in the Squeezing of a Lemon*
N. J. DAWOOD (TRANS.) · *The Seven Voyages of Sindbad the Sailor*
ISAK DINESEN · *The Dreaming Child*
SIR ARTHUR CONAN DOYLE · *The Man with the Twisted Lip*
DICK FRANCIS · *Racing Classics*
SIGMUND FREUD · *Five Lectures on Psycho-Analysis*
KAHLIL GIBRAN · *Prophet, Madman, Wanderer*
STEPHEN JAY GOULD · *Adam's Navel*
ALASDAIR GRAY · *Five Letters from an Eastern Empire*
GRAHAM GREENE · *Under the Garden*
JAMES HERRIOT · *Seven Yorkshire Tales*
PATRICIA HIGHSMITH · *Little Tales of Misogyny*
M. R. JAMES AND R. L. STEVENSON · *The Haunted Dolls' House*
RUDYARD KIPLING · *Baa Baa, Black Sheep*
PENELOPE LIVELY · *A Long Night at Abu Simbel*
KATHERINE MANSFIELD · *The Escape*

PENGUIN 60s

READ MORE IN PENGUIN

For complete information about books available from Penguin and how to order them, please write to us at the appropriate address below. Please note that for copyright reasons the selection of books varies from country to country.

IN THE UNITED KINGDOM: Please write to *Dept. JC, Penguin Books Ltd, FREEPOST, West Drayton, Middlesex UB7 0BR.*
If you have any difficulty in obtaining a title, please send your order with the correct money, plus ten per cent for postage and packaging, to *PO Box No. 11, West Drayton, Middlesex UB7 0BR.*

IN THE UNITED STATES: Please write to *Consumer Sales, Penguin USA, P.O. Box 999, Dept. 17109, Bergenfield, New Jersey 07621-0120.* VISA and MasterCard holders call 1-800-253-6476 to order all Penguin titles.

IN CANADA: Please write to *Penguin Books Canada Ltd, 10 Alcorn Avenue, Suite 300, Toronto, Ontario M4V 3B2.*

IN AUSTRALIA: Please write to *Penguin Books Australia Ltd, P.O. Box 257, Ringwood, Victoria 3134.*

IN NEW ZEALAND: Please write to *Penguin Books (NZ) Ltd, Private Bag 102902, North Shore Mail Centre, Auckland 10.*

IN INDIA: Please write to *Penguin Books India Pvt Ltd, 706 Eros Apartments, 56 Nehru Place, New Delhi 110 019.*

IN THE NETHERLANDS: Please write to *Penguin Books Netherlands bv, Postbus 3507, NL-1001 AH Amsterdam.*

IN GERMANY: Please write to *Penguin Books Deutschland GmbH, Metzlerstrasse 26, 60594 Frankfurt am Main.*

IN SPAIN: Please write to *Penguin Books S. A., Bravo Murillo 19, 1o B, 28015 Madrid.*

IN ITALY: Please write to *Penguin Italia s.r.l., Via Felice Casati 20, I-20124 Milano.*

IN FRANCE: Please write to *Penguin France S. A., 17 rue Lejeune, F-31000 Toulouse.*

IN JAPAN: Please write to *Penguin Books Japan, Ishikiribashi Building, 2-5-4, Suido, Bunkyo-ku, Tokyo 112.*

IN GREECE: Please write to *Penguin Hellas Ltd, Dimocritou 3, GR-106 71 Athens.*

IN SOUTH AFRICA: Please write to *Longman Penguin Southern Africa (Pty) Ltd, Private Bag X08, Bertsham 2013.*